A TIGER AT THE DOOR

by Audrey Huff
illustrated by Alan Flinn

Harcourt
SCHOOL PUBLISHERS

Printed in China

ISBN 10: 0-15-351501-5
ISBN 13: 978-0-15-351501-9

Ordering Options
ISBN 10: 0-15-351213-X (Grade 3 Advanced Collection)
ISBN 13: 978-0-15-351213-1 (Grade 3 Advanced Collection)
ISBN 10: 0-15-358091-7 (package of 5)
ISBN 13: 978-0-15-358091-8 (package of 5)

4 5 6 7 8 9 10 0940 12 11 10 09

Long, long ago, deep in the heart of India, a family lived in a small house at the edge of the jungle. Bright birds flitted through the thick trees of the jungle, their songs echoing through the leaves. The dense greenery below rustled as the creatures of the jungle crept past wildflowers and fruit that added splashes of color to the green carpet. It was a beautiful place, but a dangerous one.

"Be careful in the jungle," warned Mother. "The cunning tigers lie there waiting for children like you to make a mistake."

"We're careful," Anju and Sanjay promised time and again.

One spring, Father left the family to go look for work in the city. Everything was quiet and fine until one afternoon when Mother called the children in from playing.

"Our neighbor is sick," said Mother. "I must go help her. While I'm gone, you must not play in the jungle or let any strangers into the house. Do you promise?"

"We promise," agreed Anju and Sanjay. They knew the rules and always followed them carefully.

Mother packed a basket of sweet, ripe mangoes to take to their neighbor. She embraced the children, then left. Anju and Sanjay watched and waved to Mother until she was out of sight.

Little did they know that someone else was watching, too. Avinashi, a sly tiger, lurked in the grass at the edge of the jungle, watching the house.

"Look at those nice, tender children," thought the tiger. "I think I'll pay a visit to that house."

Now Avinashi knew that the children would never let a tiger into the house. She looked around for something to hide her stripes. She carefully padded around the outside of the house until she saw a large, bright square of cloth hanging from a tree. Mother had just dyed it a beautiful rose color, and she had left it there to dry.

"Aha!" said Avinashi. "I'll wrap myself in that cloth and come to the door disguised as a lady. Of course the children will let me in."

The tiger swirled the cloth all around her body, over her face, and then she padded toward the door of the house.

Knock! Knock! Knock!

"We mustn't answer the door," said Anju. "Remember, we promised."

Avinashi knocked again, but still no one came to the door. The clever tiger cleared her throat and loudly said, "Oh, children, I am a friend of your mother's. She sent me to look after you. Please let me in."

Anju and Sanjay hesitated for a moment. It would not be strange for mother to send someone to look after them.

"How do we know you are a friend of our mother's?" asked Sanjay suspiciously.

"Look at me," said Avinashi. "I am wearing a beautiful dress made from a cloth your mother gave me. Don't you recognize it?"

The children looked outside. Indeed, the figure was dressed in a cloth the same color their mother had used that afternoon.

"I suppose she must be telling the truth," whispered Anju.

"Mother would only give that cloth to a friend," agreed Sanjay.

They carefully opened the door, and Avinashi stepped inside. The crafty tiger slunk into the shadows near the door.

"Oh, my eyes!" she moaned. "Children, is there a dark room where I can sit? My eyes cannot stand too much light."

Anju and Sanjay wanted to help Mother's friend, so they led Avinashi to a cool, dark sitting room. "Such good children." sighed Avinashi. Her stomach rumbled hungrily as she peered at the children with glittering, golden eyes.

Little did the tiger know that as Anju had led Avinashi into the room, Anju had felt the fur on the tiger's paws and became suspicious.

"Dear lady, you have such thick fur on your hands," Anju said, trying to sound calm.

"Those are my gloves," said Avinashi. "I am from the city where fur gloves are all the fashion."

"Your nails are so long and sharp," said Anju. "Is that the fashion also?"

"Yes, it is," said Avinashi.

"Is it the fashion to paint stripes on your face, too?" asked Anju.

"Oh, of course," said the tiger. "The royal ladies are all wearing stripes."

Sanjay gripped Anju's hand and secretly pointed to the floor. Anju looked down and saw a long tail swishing out from under the cloth. Both of their hearts sank as they realized the terrible mistake they had made—they had let a tiger into the house!

"Won't you come sit with me?" Avinashi asked in a sweet voice.

Anju thought quickly. "Dear lady, if you don't mind, I must make dinner for my little brother. He becomes very upset when he's hungry."

Sanjay immediately began to howl. The last thing Avinashi wanted was a lot of noise that might draw attention from passersby.

"Do what you must," sighed Avinashi.

"Of course, I would be delighted to make something for you as well, honored guest," said Anju.

Avinashi smiled. "Why, I suppose a little snack before dinner would be nice. Thank you, child."

Anju grabbed Sanjay's hand, and they ran into the kitchen. Anju took every dried pepper she could find, and she began to smash and grind the brittle, fiery chilies.

"You look like such nice, healthy children," called out Avinashi. "Your mother must be a wonderful cook."

"Oh, she is," replied Anju. "She has taught us well, too." Anju filled a bowl almost to the brim with the powdered peppers. Then she poured some boiling water on them and stirred it all up. She walked towards Avinashi, carrying the bowl.

"Here, dear lady," Anju said, placing the bowl in the tiger's big, furry paws. "It is a lovely sweet soup for a spring night."

The greedy tiger eagerly began to lap up the soup. However, within seconds, the hot peppers burned her teeth, gums, and tongue. She screamed, and then she turned and crashed through the wall. Avinashi didn't stop running until she was high in the mountains, where she could cool her mouth off in the snow.

The children told Mother the story when she returned home that night and apologized for breaking their promise. Never again would they disobey her, for the lady who was a tiger nearly taught them a real lesson about the dangers of the jungle.

Think Critically

1. How is this story like *Lon Po Po*? How is it different?

2. Where do Anju and Sanjay live?

3. What first causes Anju to suspect that their visitor is a tiger?

4. What lesson did Anju and Sanjay learn?

5. Would you have let the "visitor" into the house? Why or why not?

 Language Arts

Tiger Tale Twist How else might the children have gotten the tiger out of the house? Write a new ending to this story.

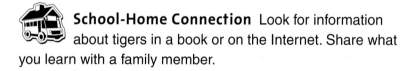 **School-Home Connection** Look for information about tigers in a book or on the Internet. Share what you learn with a family member.

Word Count: 1,058